THE RAMBLE SHAMBLE CHILDREN

CHRISTINA SOONTORNVAT

illustrated by CALDECOTT HONOR WINNER
LAUREN CASTILLO

Nancy Paulsen Books

Nancy Paulsen Books
An imprint of Penguin Random House LLC, New York

Text copyright © 2021 by Christina Soontornvat • Illustrations copyright © 2021 by Lauren Castillo • Penguin supports copyright.
Copyright fuels creativity, encourages diverse voices, promotes free speech, and creates a vibrant culture. Thank you for buying an authorized edition
of this book and for complying with copyright laws by not reproducing, scanning, or distributing any part of it in any form without permission.
You are supporting writers and allowing Penguin to continue to publish books for every reader. • Nancy Paulsen Books is a trademark of Penguin
Random House LLC. • Visit us online at penguinrandomhouse.com
Library of Congress Cataloging-in-Publication Data • Names: Soontornvat, Christina, author. | Castillo, Lauren, illustrator. • Title: The ramble shamble
children / Christina Soontornvat; illustrated by Lauren Castillo. • Description: New York: Nancy Paulsen Books, [2021] | Summary: "Five siblings
worry that their shabby old house isn't 'proper' enough, but come to see that it's perfect just the way it is"—Provided by publisher. •
Identifiers: LCCN 2019054075 | ISBN 9780399176326 (hardcover) | ISBN 9780399545825 (ebook) | ISBN 9780399545849 (ebook) •
Subjects: CYAC: Brothers and sisters—Fiction. | Family life—Fiction. | Dwellings—Maintenance and repair—Fiction. •
Classification: LCC PZ7.1.S677 Ram 2021 | DDC [E]—dc23
LC record available at https://lccn.loc.gov/2019054075
Manufactured in China by RR Donnelley Asia Printing Solutions Ltd. • ISBN 9780399176326 • 10 9 8 7 6 5 4 3 2 1 •
Design by Eileen Savage • Text set in Veronika LT Std.
The illustrations for this book were created by combining ink drawings and Gelli monoprints in Adobe Photoshop.

For Peggy—C.S.

For the 5 little Sharps
and their rad parents—L.C.

Down the mountain, across the creek,
past the last curve in the road,
five children lived together
in a ramble shamble house.

There was always work to do at
the ramble shamble house.
Merra took care of the garden,
while Locky and Roozle chased off
the always-hungry blackbirds.
Finn fed the chickens,
and Jory looked after the mud.

There were always meals to share at
the ramble shamble house.
Merra picked the salad,
while Locky and Roozle pulled the carrots.
Finn fetched the eggs,
and Jory looked after the mud.

The garden always needed digging or weeding
or gathering up.
There were always bugs to catch or fences to patch.
The work was hardly ever done, but doing it
together made it easier.

At night, when the children were full and sleepy, they
all piled into Merra's bed and listened to her spin stories
about giants and dragons and brave explorers.

One afternoon, the children took a break to
read a book they had found in the attic.

"Oh, that's what a proper house looks like,"
said Merra. "And what a pretty garden."

"Looks nice," said Finn.

"Definitely doesn't look like ours," said Roozle.

"But maybe it could," said Locky.

The next day, the children set to
work turning the ramble shamble
house into a proper home.

They propered up the chickens.

They propered up
a scarecrow.

They raked over all the mud puddles
because mud definitely isn't proper.

They propered up the garden.
"Proper houses always have roses," said Locky.
"We can pull up the carrots to make room
for them," said Roozle.

"Perfect," said Merra. "Now all that's
missing is the proper finishing touch."

"We must have a proper chandelier," said Merra.
"I think they're made of diamonds."
"This stinkbug is *shaped* like a diamond," said Locky.
"We've got plenty of those," said Roozle.

When they were finished, everything
looked more proper.

But things were not quite right.

"Aah!" shrieked Merra. "One of the chickens laid an egg in my shoe!"

"Guess they didn't like the proper henhouse I made," said Finn.

"I can't pick any peas," said Locky. "The rosebushes keep scratching me up."

"The chandelier is flying away!" shouted Roozle.

"This isn't proper at all," groaned Merra.

"Hold on," said Finn. "Has anyone seen Jory?"
"Isn't he in the mud puddle?" said Locky.
"Oh no! We propered it up!"

"We have to find him before it gets dark,"
said Merra, swallowing back tears.
As they entered the forest, the children

"What if a giant stole Jory?" whispered Locky.

"Or a dragon?" said Roozle.

"There's no such thing," said Merra. "Here, Finn, you go first."

They followed the trail through a dark tunnel of

"JORY!"

That's when Jory took his very
first steps, straight into the arms of
his ramble shamble family.

That night, the children sat together on the porch, munching snap peas. They had put everything back the way it was—especially the mud.

"Our house sure doesn't look like the one in the picture," said Roozle.

"It's ramble shamble," said Locky.

"It's ours," said Finn.

Merra smiled. "It's perfect."

The children stayed up late,
watching Jory make a proper mess.
While the stars shone overhead,
brighter than diamonds.